Felicia Tales

The Many Misadventures of Felicia Brown

A Trip to the Vet

By M. Deborah Bowden

Published by Harp Tree Publishing

ISBN: 978-0-9968677-2-6
Illustrated by Savannah Horton

Mission Statement

The Felicia Brown series is for 6 to 9 year olds and contains learning situations—acts and consequences. The stories lend themselves to discussions between a child and an adult. The books are separate stories and can be read in any order. A few more advanced words are added to increase vocabulary. A word / definition matchup is included to aid understanding.

Dedication

These stories are based on the ones my father wrote for me as a child. I always loved the antics of Felicia, Discrepancy, and Atrocious. In turn, I told these stories to my daughter. She insisted that I write them for other children to enjoy. Therefore, I dedicate this and other Felicia books to my father, Bradley Garrison Patrick who sometimes wrote articles under his pseudonym Angus Beefsteak, and to my daughter, Erin Bradleigh Bowden. She is also a writer and talented singer, songwriter, and musician.

I also dedicate these stories to my mentors Hank Swain and Debi Stanton. Thanks also to Thoth and Bastet.

Contents

Chapter One
Pets Gone Wild

Felicia brought out Atrocious' cat carrier. The black cat knew that meant the vet and shots. She darted up the tallest tree she could find. Felicia spotted her peeking out from the leaves. "She's up there, Daddy."

Timothy Brown leaned a ladder against the tree and climbed up. "Hope I can catch her," he said.

"I know where she'll run next. I'll go there."

Atrocious waited until he could almost reach her. She flipped her tail and waited. She jumped on his arm. She ran to his shoulder. She raced down his back and leg to the ground.

She sped to her next hiding place. Felicia was waiting. She grabbed Atrocious before she disappeared into the small barn.

"Gotcha," Felicia said. "I know your hiding places, Atrocious. You can trick my daddy, but not me." The cat growled but didn't struggle.

Mr. Brown left to doctor his wounds. Felicia put Atrocious in her carrier, and found her father.

"I caught Atrocious, Daddy. Gee, she really hurt you this time."

Her mother Mattie dabbed rubbing alcohol on his cuts.

"Let me help too." Felicia grabbed the Band-Aids.

Mattie laughed. "That's a lot of patches you stuck on him."

Timothy rolled his eyes at the both of them.

"Thanks, ladies." He eased his clothing back on. "Atrocious does this every year. Discrepancy will be worse."

Discrepancy slept on the far side of the yard. He heard Atrocious' yowling, and hurried to her. He saw his pal inside the carrier. He figured out the vet trip. He pawed at the door to open it, but spun the carrier around. Atrocious yowled louder.

Felicia popped out carrying Discrepancy's leash. His nails slid on the porch floor as he tried to escape. He tripped over the carrier. It rolled over and over.

Atrocious shrieked, "Meow, 'ow, yowl, growl." That meant, "I'm going to hurt you when I get the chance." Discrepancy landed on his face.

Felicia grabbed him and fastened the leash to his collar. She hooked the other end to the porch railing. He tried to tug his head out of his collar. He tried to break the leash by running. He choked himself both times.

He sat and yodeled. He ran around the railing post one way. Then back around the post the other way.

Chapter Two
An Idea

Felicia feared Discrepancy would hurt himself. She sat down on the steps. She put her chin in her hands and thought. She had an idea.

"Mom used alcohol on Dad's cuts," she said to her pets. "Daddy sometimes says he needs alcohol to calm his nerves. Then he can relax after work. That's what you need, Discrepancy. Then you can relax."

Felicia slipped inside her parents' liquor closet. She grabbed an open bottle of whiskey.

"I know I'm not supposed to get in here. But this is really important. I have to calm my dog down. He hates the vet. It'll help Daddy too and Dr. Swan."

Felicia took the bottle outside and climbed on top of Discrepancy. She locked his head between her knees. She stuck the bottle in his mouth, and poured.

Her dog didn't have a choice. He either swallowed or drowned. Some spilled, but she got a lot down his throat.

His eyes bugged out. He sneezed. He shook his head. He burped. He hiccupped. He sat down and opened and shut his eyes. He saw everything double. He was very quiet.

"I think Atrocious needs some too."

She pulled her cat out of the carrier. Felicia held her like a baby and poured. Most of it spilled on her fur, but some went down.

Felicia returned her to the carrier. Atrocious tried to spit it up like a hairball. But the whiskey stayed down. She licked her wet fur, growling with each taste.

Felicia hid the bottle underneath the car seat. "I'll keep this in case my pets need more to relax."

Chapter Three
Dad Is Troubled

Mr. Brown came outside. He was surprised to see how calm the pets were. He figured he'd have to half-drag, half-carry Discrepancy to the car. Then listen to Discrepancy groan and Atrocious scream the whole trip.

Something was wrong. He gave his daughter a thoughtful look. Felicia smiled sweetly and put the pets in the back. She jumped into the front seat and off they went.

During the trip, Timothy glanced often at Felicia. He wondered what she'd done. Knowing his daughter, she was up to *something. And that meant trouble.*

"I'll go sign us in," Timothy said when they arrived. "You get the carrier out."

When her dad returned, Felicia said, "You carry kitty. I'll lead Discrepancy."

He said, "Well, okay. I figured Discrepancy would knock you down, but he seems calm." Timothy watched the dog as Felicia led him inside. "Is he leaning against you?"

Felicia didn't say anything. They sat down on the wrap-around seat in the waiting room. Timothy looked at the cat. "Is she sleeping?" Felicia just smiled.

Timothy petted the dog's shoulder. Discrepancy's head floated around. The dog looked at his owner, but the hand petting him looked like several hands. "Discrepancy, you look like you're half asleep," he said.

Chapter Four
With Dr. Swan

Mary, a helper, called their names. Timothy stared at the way Discrepancy walked down the hall. He lifted each foot up high, and then put it down carefully. He didn't walk straight. He stilled and leaned on Felicia.

Mary said, "We need both your pets' weights. Let's start with Atrocious."

Felicia pulled Atrocious from the carrier. She stood the cat on the scale. Her four legs slid out in all four directions. She flattened down like a bear-skin rug.

Mary said, "Fifteen pounds. Please put her on the table."

"Let me lift her," Timothy said. "She might claw." He reached around her middle. She folded it in half. Atrocious hissed, but didn't scratch. Her head and legs just flopped.

He put her on the table, and she flattened out. He picked her up and tried again. She flattened out again. She hissed and hiccupped. Her tongue hung out.

Timothy turned to demand an explanation from Felicia. Before he could, Dr. Swan walked in.

"I see Atrocious agreed to go first." He turned to his helper, "Mary, it's getting busy out front, you go help. I'm okay here." Mary smiled and left.

Dr. Swan checked Atrocious' teeth, tongue, and ears. He listened to her heart and lungs. He checked her fur and paws. "Did you give her a something before you came in?" Dr. Swan asked. "It usually takes two people to hold her."

Timothy shook his head. Felicia smiled, but didn't say a word.

"Well, she's much easier to check today. Let's get her temperature while she's quiet," Dr. Swan said.

Timothy lifted her up so Dr. Swan could use the thermometer. Atrocious hissed and growled—thermometers were worse than shots! She tried to claw, but scratched the air because she saw two doctors. She attacked the wrong one.

Dr. said, "Her temperature's normal and her eyes are clear. Just a little foggy. Hmm." He picked up the needle to give her a shot.

Shots made Atrocious fighting mad. She squalled. She tried to bite and claw anyone she could reach. Her feet slid out from under her. She rolled onto her back--her paws in the air.

Dr. Swan frowned. He checked her eyes again. He sniffed her fur. "She smells like alcohol!"

"Uh-oh, gotta do something quick," Felicia said under her breath. "I'll get Discrepancy's weight, Daddy."

She tried to pull him, but he couldn't stand up. She tried to lift up his bottom, but his front legs slid forward. She grabbed his legs and pulled him toward the scales. She turned him around and lifted his hips onto the scales.

She tripped and stepped on Discrepancy's tail. He squealed and jumped. Felicia landed on top of him. Discrepancy pulled himself up as she rolled off.

He crashed into Mr. Brown. He knocked him into the table where Atrocious sat. It was on wheels and banged into the wall. Atrocious leaped off the table and landed on Dr. Swan's back. All her claws were out.

Mary heard the noise and burst through the door. She rammed into Dr. Swan. Atrocious squalled and climbed up Mary's lab coat to her shoulder. It was as high as she could get.

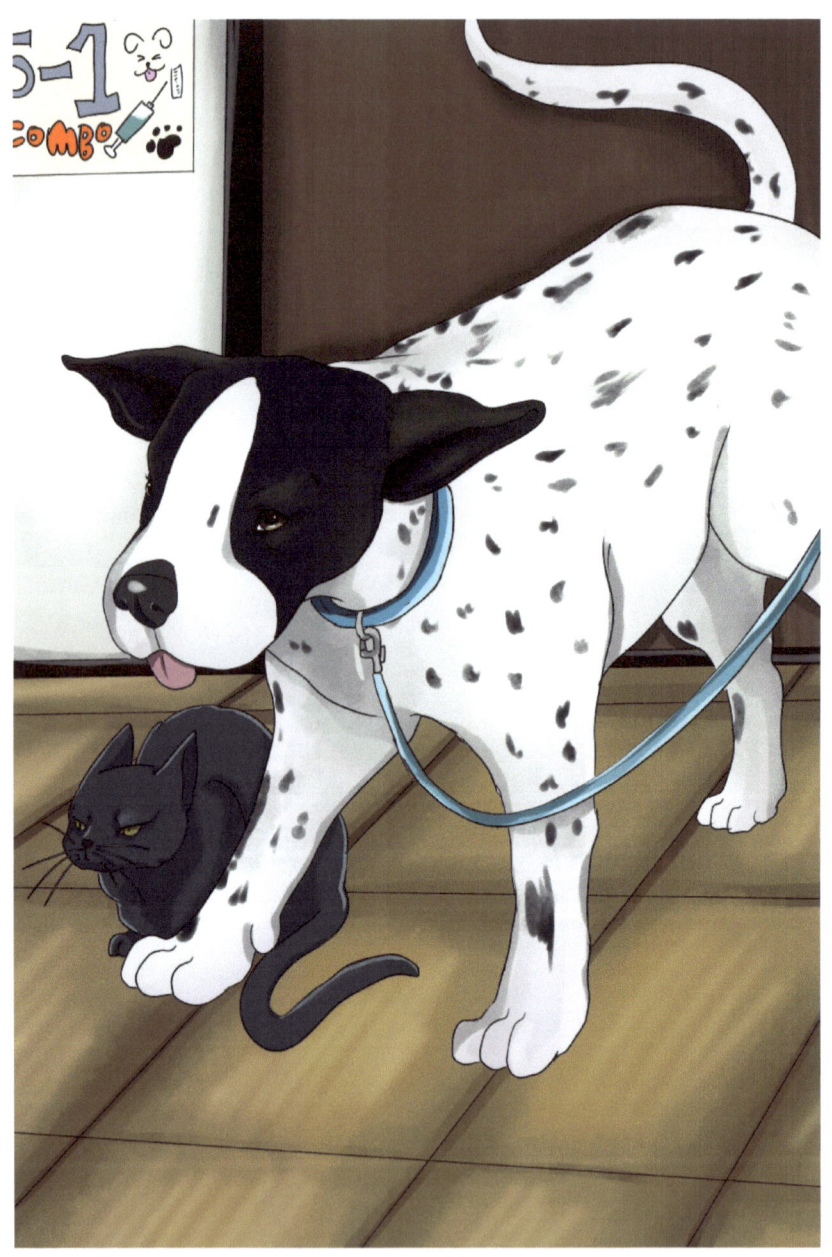

Chapter Five
The Great Escape

Mary yelled. That scared Atrocious. She trusted Discrepancy and jumped on his back. She held on tight as he escaped out the door. The dogs in the back pens heard the racket. They barked over and over.

Discrepancy thought the dogs were after them. He bumped down the hall as fast as he could. Many pets and owners out front heard the noises. The door burst open. A cat riding a dog charged in.

Discrepancy crashed into a St. Bernard and his owner at the check-in window.

Atrocious flew over Discrepancy's head. She landed on the huge dog's rear. She dug in her claws.

The St. Bernard spun around and around. He rammed into two Labradors and a lady holding a Poodle. The Poodle's high-pitched yapping alarmed the Labs. They stood up.

The little dog leaped off the lady. It ran around and around the Labradors and the

St. Bernard. All their leashes tangled up. They struggled and tugged in different directions. Atrocious fell off Discrepancy. He found a corner and hid.

The St. Bernard yanked his owner into the pile. Three men jumped to save her as she fell. The dogs tripped the men. Two of them fell to the floor with the lady on top.

The third man dropped near the Poodle's owner. She shrieked, "My baby, my baby, save my baby!

Her shrieking scared Atrocious. She sped across the pile of dogs and people. She plopped on a woman with two

Siamese. They attacked Atrocious. The woman screamed. She knocked the warring cats to the floor.

They landed on Discrepancy. He saw four angry Siamese attacking two Atrociouses.

He barked and growled to save his pal. Atrocious hid under him. The Siamese battled each other all across the room.

They fought by a gentleman holding a bird cage. He couldn't calm his nervous parrot. The bird forced its cage open. It flew around and around over everyone's head, screaming, "Bad boy! Bad boy!"

Chapter Six
All hands on Deck

Dr. Swan, three helpers, Timothy, and Felicia rushed into the room.

Felicia dragged Discrepancy back down the hall. Mr. Brown grabbed Atrocious. She was too tired to claw him.

Two helpers untangled the dogs. One put the lady and her Siamese in another room. Dr. Swan got the parrot into its cage. Then he returned to Atrocious and Discrepancy.

Dr. Swan checked the dog and gave him his shots. He asked Felicia. "Did you give your pets alcohol? They're drunk."

Felicia said, "Yes, I wanted them (Relaxed) calm. They hate coming here. I guess I didn't give them enough. I'll give them more next time."

"Oh, no, Felicia," Dr. Swan said. "You had the right idea but the wrong stuff. Have your father get calming pills next time. I'll give them shots to help with the effects of the alcohol. Only give them water for the next 24 hours."

Chapter Seven
Home

When Felicia and Timothy returned to the car, he asked, "What did you give them?"

Felicia pulled out the three-quarters empty bottle of whiskey from under the seat.

"Here, Daddy, there's some left if you want to calm your nerves."

"Never get in my liquor closet again. I'll lock it from now on. Just in case you try that again. No TV for a week. We'll talk about why when we get home."

"But Daddy, Dr. Swan said I had the right idea. I relaxed Discrepancy and Atrocious. I was trying to help. I didn't want you to get scratched more. It was easier for Dr. Swan to give their shots too."

Timothy groaned. "Your pets will be very sick soon. It's your job to care for them all by yourself. No short-cuts. Do you understand?"

"Yes, Daddy, would a pain-killer help?"

"Felicia! Only water."

"Okay," smiled the little red head. Her mind thinking up more ideas.

Watch for more adventures with Felicia, Atrocious, and Discrepancy coming soon!

Vocabulary

These words are for older grades.

Do you know what they mean?
Match them with their meaning.

A. Alcohol (4), Liquor (5), Whiskey (6)   1. Heat

B. Growl, Shriek, Squall, Yowl (4)   2. Tool

C. Relax (4)   3. Drinks

D. Scratch (4)   4. Calm

E. Temperature (4)   5. Noises

F. Thermometer (6)   6. Claw

Reading Comprehension
and
Opinion Questions
with Answers

Below are possible questions which can be used to gauge a child's understanding of the story, if so desired. Some require a child's opinion. Opinions can engage a conversation.

Some or all may be asked or others substituted. This is NOT a test.

1. **What is the problem Felicia and her father are having with Discrepancy and Atrocious?**
   Possible answers:
   - The pets hate going to the vet.
   - They are afraid of the shots, thermometers, and check-ups
   - They are very nervous.
   - They are trying to run away or hide.

   Accept other reasonable answers.

2. **How does Felicia get the idea to give the pets alcohol?**
   Possible answers:
   - She watched her mother put alcohol on her father's scratches.
   - She remembered her father saying he drank alcohol to calm his nerves or relax.

3. Why did she give the pets alcohol?

Possible opinions:

- She thought if the alcohol relaxed her father, it would do the same for the pets.
- She was worried that the pets would hurt themselves because of their fear.
- She thought a calm cat wouldn't scratch her father or Dr. Swan and his helpers.
- She felt relaxed pets would be easier to give exams or shots.

Accept other opinions.

4. Why didn't she follow her father's rule to stay out of the liquor closet?

Possible opinions:

- She felt helping her pets and her father and Dr. Swan was more important.
- She couldn't think of any other way to solve her pets' fears.
- She didn't think her parents had any ideas to help.

Accept other opinions.

5. What problems happened because she gave her pets alcohol?

Possible answers:

- The pets couldn't help themselves or think.
- They became more afraid.
- They caused all sorts of disasters in the entire building.
- They were going to be very sick soon.

Accept other reasonable answers.

6. What punishment did her father give Felicia?
Possible answers:
- She couldn't watch TV for a week.
- She had to take care of her pets while they were sick all by herself.

Accept other reasonable answers.

7. A. Do you think Felicia learned her lesson?
Possible Opinions:

A. No. She tried to argue with her father.

No. She wanted to give them pain-killers instead of just water.

B. Will she learn after seeing how sick the pets will become?
Possible Opinions:

No. She was thinking up more ideas and smiling.

Yes, maybe. Her father was going to explain why pets shouldn't have alcohol.

Accept other opinions.

Yes, no, maybe---give reasons

Author Mary Deborah Bowden

Author Deborah Bowden first developed a love of story-telling and writing from her father, Bradley Garrison Patrick, when she was very young. She was a story-teller long before she began writing her tales in the 1970s. She especially enjoys writing about animals for children.

She taught English and creative writing in the public schools and college for 25 years before retiring to rear her daughter, Erin Bradleigh, on whom she honed her talents.

She has been in love with Brown County, Indiana since her college friends enticed her here in early 1970—she knew she had found her home.

She was a member of the Bartholomew County Writer's Group, Mill Race Senior Scribes in Columbus, and the Writers, Readers, and Poets Society of Brown County. When not writing, she enjoys the trees and hills around her Brown County home.

She is the author of these adult books: *Dandelions and other Weeds: A Collection of Musings, Memories, Songs, Poems, and Stories; Pat and Little Pat: A Slightly Unconventional Cookbook from a Dad and Daughter; Little Lestoil Ladies: the Cream of Premium Dolls and*

How to Identify Them; Daylilies and Nightshades, a sequel to her Dandelions book;

Additionally, her books, *Kudzu Beyond Control* and *30 Hydes,* both horror novels, are written under her pen name, Rosemary Coven.

Her works for children include: *The Sack Lunch,* illustrated by her talented daughter;

The Mr. Bramble Bones series: *Mr. Bramble Bones Is Too Cold to Play; Mr. Bramble Bones and Grimmy Share a Home; Mr. Bramble Bones and Grimmy in The Case of the Missing Blue Blanket; Mr. Bramble Bones and Grimmy Clean Up; Mr. Bramble Bones and Grimmy in A Christmas to Remember; Mr. Bramble Bones and Grimmy and The Ghost Hunters.*

The Horus the Buzzard series: *Horus, the Misunderstood Buzzard: Horus Has a Problem; Horus the Misunderstood Buzzard: Moonbeam is Different; Horus the Misunderstood Buzzard in Snickers Has a Toothache; Horus the Misunderstood Buzzard in Tid-Bit Has a Secret*

The Felicia Tales series: *Many Misadventures of Felicia Brown in Felicia and the Groundhog's Day Misadventure.*

Ms. Bowden has contributed articles and stories to *The Reflection Rag,* a quarterly publication, *Pen-It Magazine* for writers, *The Realm,* an online magazine of the paranormal, and The Pen and Pulpit Magazine.

Her writings appeared in *Kairos: 1970; Midwest Poets from Pen to Paper; Treasured Moments, Hillsounds III, The Wishing Well: Discoveries,*

She has read her short stories on radio, and is also a lyricist with her songs appearing on the CD, *Been and Done,* in a collaboration.

Look for new books in all three children's series coming soon as well as a new horror novel on Amazon.com.

www.ingramcontent.com/pod-product-compliance
Lightning Source LLC
Chambersburg PA
CBHW041031170626
46815CB00001B/49